SOMETHING DELICIOUS

Jill Lewis ✳ Ali Pye

EGMONT

The Guzzler had been eating all day.

He had munched breakfast, crunched elevenses, chomped twelveses, and guzzled the most enormous lunch.

But he was still looking
for a *little something* . . .

"I know where I can find a little something,"
said the greedy Guzzler, and he licked his lips
thinking of the feast that lay ahead.

"There are lots
of Little Somethings
in the cave on the hill."

Inside the cave on the hill,
all the Little Somethings
were very worried.

"The Guzzler is coming!
RUN!" they cried.
But it was too late.

The Little Somethings
quivered and **quaked**.
They couldn't think what to do.

"Don't worry, everybody," said Miniwiggler. "Lots of other things are little.

Maybe the Guzzler would like one of these instead of one of us."

Until *one of them* had a good idea.

And he pulled out a perfect little **glob** fruit.

The Guzzler soon spotted
the delicious little glob fruit.
"OOOH!" he said.
"What luck!" And he ate it.

GULP!

Then he looked up.

"Now, what was I doing? Oh, yes!
I was looking for a Little Something. Hmmm.
I think it should be a plump Little Something."

"Thank goodness," said a skinny Little Something, "that's *me* safe. No one could call me plump."

And all the other skinny Little Somethings breathed a huge sigh of relief.

But the plump Little Somethings shivered and shook.

Then clever Miniwiggler had another good idea.

"Lots of little things are plump," he said. "Maybe the Guzzler would like a plump little lush ball instead of a plump Little Something?"

So Miniwiggler and his plump little friend Skidaddler pushed a lush ball up onto the middle of a rock.

The Guzzler soon spotted it.
"OOOH!" he said.
"What luck!" And he ate it.

GULP!

Then he looked up.

"Now, what was I doing?
Oh, yes! I was looking
for a plump Little Something.
Hmmm. I think it should be
a plump Little Something with
no wings or nasty stings."

"What a relief!" said
a Little Something with wings.
"I thought I was a gonner."

And all the Little Somethings with wings
or stings breathed a huge sigh of relief.

Now there were only two Little Somethings left to choose from. They were little and plump, with no wings or stings.

Miniwiggler and Skidaddler looked at one another. EEK!

The Guzzler soon spotted them.

"AHA!"

he shouted. "What luck!"

And he picked up Skidaddler.

Down on the ground,
Miniwiggler sweated and fretted.
He couldn't let this happen.
But he was almost out of ideas . . .

Miniwiggler cried at the top of his brave little voice.

The Guzzler dropped Skidaddler and stared at Miniwiggler.

"WHAT DID YOU SAY?"

he growled.

Miniwiggler squirmed and squiggled but he yelled loudly, "LEAVE US ALONE!"

The Guzzler smiled and licked his lips.

"YOU are exactly what I want," he said.
"A plump Little Something with no wings or stings.

". . . to come with me to Normous Nosh's **birthday feast!** You'll be my guest."

"Why me?"
asked Miniwiggler.

"Because you are little and won't eat as much as a Big Something," replied the Guzzler, "so there will be much more for me! HA! HA!

And everyone will like you because you don't have wings or nasty stings . . . and you're plump like the rest of us."

To Normous Nosh's cave

So Miniwiggler went to the birthday feast at Normous Nosh's cave.
And he had the time of his life!

He had never seen *so* much to eat.

Even the greedy Big Somethings couldn't
finish it all. Which was lucky, really . . .

. . . because that meant there was
a *little something* left for Miniwiggler
to take home for his friends.

NOSH BISCUITS

Now **you** can try this recipe for a very tasty *little something* from the feast!

You will need:
- To ask your own Big Something to help you
- To heat the oven to 200°C or gas mark 6
- To wash your hands

Now fetch:
- A big and a little bowl
- A fork, a teaspoon, a tablespoon and a spoon for mixing
- A greased baking tray
- 200g plain flour
- 1 heaped teaspoon baking powder
- 75g butter or margarine
- 1 tablespoon Demerara sugar
- 50g chocolate chips
- 1 or 2 bananas, mashed
- 1 teaspoon lemon juice
- 1 large egg, beaten

What you do:
1. In the big bowl, rub butter into the flour and baking powder.
2. Stir in sugar and chocolate chips.
3. In the little bowl, mash banana(s) with the lemon juice then add the egg.
4. Tip the little bowl's ingredients into the big bowl and beat together.
5. Place 10 heaps of the mixture onto the greased tray.
6. Bake in oven for 15 minutes.

To the chef: These are mainly for Little Somethings to eat. But perhaps a Big Something is allowed one or two.

THE BIG SOMETHING BISCUIT TESTERS
Swoop
Trufflestumper
Normous Nosh
Hoovle
Plumpenstein
Guzzler

A SPOTTER GUIDE TO THE
little
SoMETHINGS

Spike Fox

Bob

Skidaddler

Miniwiggler

Little Hogwash

Snaggles

Quiff

Star

Twiglittle

Sparky

Stingle

Crackle

Bunnikins

Trunky

Spring Chicken